Magic Even You Can Do
by *BLAST*

. . . .

~Charles Holdefer~

Illustrated by Royce M. Becker

Sagging Shorts

ISBN: 978-1-944697-72-3 (paperback)
Library of Congress Control Number: 2018962865

Sagging Meniscus Press
saggingmeniscus.com

About the Author

....

Blast has been amazing people for years. On five continents, for crowned heads, for international celebrities and ordinary folk, he has been an ongoing source of wonder. Institutions can't hold him. His record for the world's longest card trick still stands. Now this famous manipulator offers you a choice selection of his most delightful magic tricks, all carefully explained and simplified with the beginner in mind. You need not practice for hours. This is magic even you can do!

About the Manuscript

This manuscript was found behind a radiator at a bar called La Serrurérie in Poitiers, France, along with a pair of handcuffs. On my next trip to America, I showed it to a New York literary agent who refused to touch it ("Oooh, looks greasy," he said), so I sent it directly to JS in Montclair, New Jersey, who, with the help of RB, disinfected and meticulously restored the pages and illustrations and removed an old teaspoon which was really of no consequence, to create the volume in its present form. I vouch for its accuracy. —CH

Table of Wonders

Dedication

. . . .

When one achieves greatness, modesty requires that its sources should be acknowledged.

This volume is dedicated to the memory of my mentor, Mr. Mysto, the inspired man who put me on the happy path to magic.

During the Intermission I'll say more about my youthful encounter with this great performer, but for uninitiated readers I would like to begin with a valuable piece of advice that Mr. Mysto gave me.

"Be yourself," he told me. "Be unexplainable."

This is the key to success. It animates the spirit of these pages.

So, remember:

Be yourself. Be unexplainable.

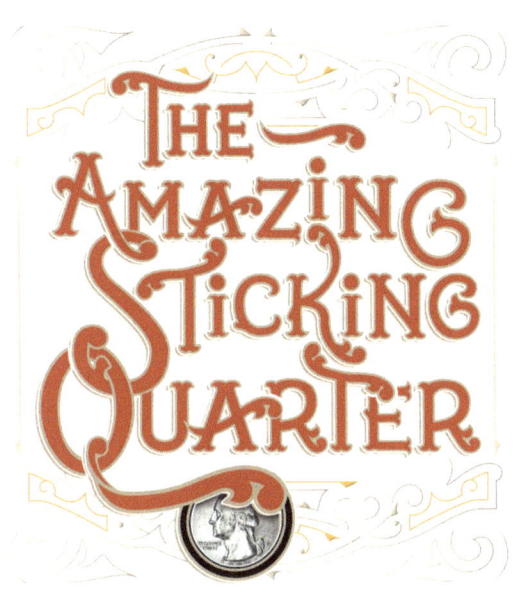

THE AMAZING STICKING QUARTER

EFFECT:

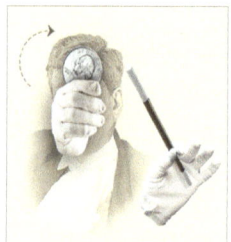

This trick never fails to startle and amuse. You display a quarter for everyone to see and, bringing it to your forehead, you make several mystic passes with your hand. After the last pass, you reveal that the quarter is stuck to your forehead.

You bow, and the quarter does not fall off. You may jump up and down, and the quarter does not fall off. You may bend over backwards across a chair, laughing and kicking, and still the quarter does not fall off.

Next, to the amazement of everyone, you may challenge members of your audience to remove the quarter. Come one and all, ladies and gentlemen, they cannot pull it off, though they tug their mightiest.

Truly, you must be a wonder worker!

METHOD:

Like many great mysteries, the secret of the quarter is ingeniously simple.

All you need is a quarter and a twopenny screw. The head of the screw is welded to the back of the quarter, an easy and inexpensive task for any metalworking shop. The screw itself can be procured for a few cents.

Display the ungimmicked face of the quarter to the audience, then bring it to your forehead. Your mystic passes should be done with a circular motion while maintaining steady contact with the coin, which facilitates the screw's entry.

Once the quarter is in place, you may indulge in any gyrations desired or submit to the collective efforts of the audience. They will never succeed because they will always try to pull the quarter *away* from you.

It will not occur to people to twist in the same plane as your head.

It's never happened to me.

Front

Side

THE INCREDIBLE TALKING GOLDFISH

EFFECT:

This trick has been known to induce stupefaction. You bring out a bowl with a goldfish in it. You set it on a table, and ask for silence. You announce that you shall hypnotize it.

After passing your fingers hypnotically around the bowl, you declare that the goldfish is now in a trance, and is ready to answer questions.

This will provoke surprise, and in some cases alarm, but it is true. "Are you ready?" you say to the bowl, and after a pause, a voice is heard, small but distinct, "Yes!"

Take any question from the audience:

"What day is it?"
The goldfish replies: "Tuesday."
Or:
"How should a person live?"
The goldfish says: "Gusto, baby, with gusto!"
Or:
"What is the capital of Manitoba?"
The goldfish: "Winnipeg."
What a smart goldfish!

METHOD:

The secret of the goldfish is a confederate hidden under the table, which should be draped. In truth it is the confederate who does all the talking, answers all the questions. Ideally this is a job for a small person, because tall tables tend to attract suspicion. It is sensible to use children as they are naturally shorter and you can pay  them less. Besides, people expect a goldfish to have a high voice.

The particular beauty of this stunt is its uncanny realism. A goldfish, without any special training or electrical shocks, will open and close its mouth at regular intervals. This contributes greatly to the illusion of speech. Moreover, goldfish are notoriously soporific; they *look* hypnotized. Both of these qualities make your job that much easier.

Lastly, try to find a clever child to be your confederate. This will be of great service for history and geography questions. But not too clever—nobody likes a wiseass goldfish.

You know what they say: folks always have a hankering for the chthonic.

And it's true. I've experimented with many tricks over the years and even some of my personal favorites like "Squeeze My Lump" and "Trapshooting an Angel" haven't gone down as well as "Devil May Care."

It's a guaranteed crowd pleaser!

Here's the story:

EFFECT:

You wheel out a giant mousetrap and slowly—*drumroll!*—you dramatically set the spring.

Next, you push out a curtain and place it in front of the mousetrap.

The tension builds as you make a hellish incantation. (Choose your personal favorite, whatever seems apposite.) In season, I like to use a holiday theme:

> *Away in a manger*
> *A reindeer is dead*
> *Poor Rudolph, my goodness!*
> *You cut off his head!*
>
> *His eyes in the fruitcake*
> *His nose for your sled*
> *The manger's a barbecue pit:*
> *Oooh, you're BAD!!*

Suddenly, the audience hears an enormous SNAP!

What can it be?

The curtain is parted, revealing . . . the Prince of the Underworld *himself!*

Method:

For this amazement you will need the help of your confederate hidden under your table with the goldfish bowl. (Remember? Keep that little fellow busy!) Have the confederate dress in a devil suit. *

After displaying the giant mousetrap, you push out the curtain. Demonstrate to the audience that there is nothing behind the curtain by opening it and closing it again. The moment you close it, your confederate takes advantage of the cover to dart out from beneath the table. He then trots alongside the curtain, out of sight, as you push it toward the mousetrap. (Sneaky devil!)

By the time the incantation reaches its climax, he has inserted his ersatz tail within striking range and can safely spring the trap without maiming himself, causing the SNAP!

As long as he hops and screams, the audience will be thrilled, and even more in awe of your prowess as you wheel away this fussy Beelzebub. You have just altered the moral balance of the cosmos!

---

* *The price of the suit can be deducted from his wages.*

1.

2.

3.

HOLY CAPPUCCINO!

(A master magician's tips on how to "live the life" at your local coffee shop)

Much of being a conjurer is acting like one. Onstage, you are in the spotlight, the focus of dreams. You are unexplainable. Words will fail!

Offstage, however, you take a different approach. You find other ways to communicate your amazingness. An aura of mystery should follow you like a sweet fragrance.

But how?

For starters, DO NOT perform part of your act in everyday settings. You should never appear to work for free or to sell yourself cheaply. •

Rather, a more subversive approach is required. This is accomplished by cultivating random strangeness and tweaking the psychic anxieties of people you meet.

For instance, at the local coffee shop!

• *When needed I sometimes supplement my income by doing consulting on Special Effects for Hollywood studios. You have probably seen my work in films like* Calliope! *and* Obese Children with Handguns II.

EFFECT & METHOD:

When you place your order, hunch your shoulders and allude to the omens of recent comets. "Looks bad. But there's still time for a double-skinny. We can thank the moons of Jupiter for that! I'd also like a muffin, please."

(Be sure to pant.)

"If death comes in a massive fireball," you ask, "how much do you think we'll feel it?"

Often, your barista will embellish the top of your cappuccino with a delicate leaf design. This adds a tasteful touch. But when your server looks away to ring up your purchase, all it takes is several deft stabs with the tip of your finger to transform the design into an astonishing copy of Edvard Munch's classic painting "The Scream."

Feign innocence as you accept your change. Then, look down at the cup. *Freeze*. Invariably the server will look down, too.

"A sign of the times," you say.

1. Served   2. Stir   3. Ooooooh!

MAGIC BEARDS

EFFECT:

This feat is psychological magic at its best. It has long been my opinion that magicians concentrate too much on visual magic—i.e., vanishes, appearances, transformations.

But the Magic Beards are different. The Magic Beards operate on another level entirely. With them, you change not visual phenomena but the personal, interior world of your audience; you actually change *moods*.

The feat unfolds as follows: You invite the members of your audience to put on beards, which you distribute. And, donning them simultaneously (this has worked under laboratory conditions), their moods begin to change. For the better!

METHOD:

The secret of the Magic Beards lies in an intrinsic quality of artificial facial hair. This quality has hitherto been underexploited in magic, as in other aspects of everyday life. Namely, donning a fake beard releases endorphins in the hypothalamus and improves a person's disposition. Complaisance or even jolliness is a frequent result and, sometimes, high-pitched laughter.

Note the emphasis on *phony* facial hair. Real beards and moustaches do not count. Indeed, some of the most disagreeable people I have ever met wear real facial hair. These people are assholes.

But a false beard confers wonderful powers to its wearer. (Often, if I'm by myself and feeling blue, I'll put on my beard and walk around the room for a while. Before long I'll feel better. I start laughing and cannot stop. Keep one in the medicine cabinet.) The only danger is the potential for abuse, applying this principle frivolously.

In public performances, with the accumulated jolliness of the entire audience, the effect is overwhelming. People roar! Fuzzy cotton beards are the best (and a surprise favorite among the ladies!). If these prove to be financially prohibitive (as I have discovered for stadium performances), paper cut-outs will suffice.

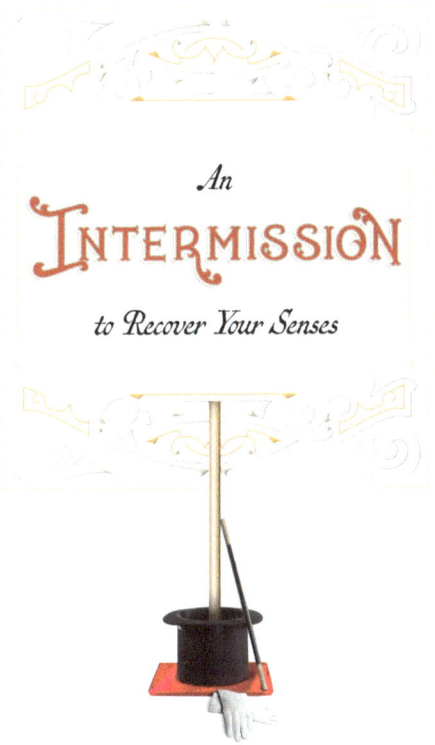

An

INTERMISSION

to Recover Your Senses

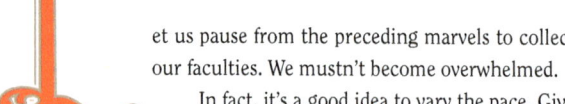

et us pause from the preceding marvels to collect our faculties. We mustn't become overwhelmed.

In fact, it's a good idea to vary the pace. Give folks a breather. I like to regale spectators with stories of my fascinating life.

Over the years I've mingled with celebrities, royalty and interesting people of all stripes. These encounters are the source of ripping good yarns which audiences love to hear. Tales of my run-ins with secret service agents (those people seem to have *a thing* against illusionists, a real chip on their pistol-strapped shoulders!) or my experience with an aspiring starlet in a spray-on leopard-skin leotard who later went on to have a successful career in network journalism. (Come to my show and I'll name the name.) But my favorite tales center on my beloved mentor, Mr. Mysto.

I first saw the man perform at the Adventureland theme park in Altoona, Iowa. It was a sweltering afternoon and he was working from a gazebo. In those days I was an untutored youth with asthma and scabs on my knees from the other children pushing me down all the time. (This is shockingly at odds with the figure I have cut in later years, but I am not ashamed to admit my past.) That day, he smiled and invited me up onto the gazebo, whereupon he pulled silver dollars out of my ears, nose and other orifices. He tore a pigeon in half with his bare hands (*oh, how the audience shuddered!*) and then he restored it. At one point, I'll always remember, he responded so ferociously to a heckler that parents clapped their hands over the ears of their children.

This made a great impression on a lad like myself. Mr. Mysto opened me up to a new world of possibility.

True, Mysto's career was marked by ups and downs. Critics carp about his wilderness years, his susceptibility to criticism, his parole violations. But this much is true: whatever the venue, from rock festivals to teamsters' conventions to scout jamborees, he was always true to his art. I know this first-hand because for a brief time during my teens, I was lucky enough to be his apprentice and join Mysto on the road.

One gig I'll always remember was at an Arctic weather station in Greenland for a small encampment of climate scientists, polymer engineers and CIA men. They were hungry for entertainment, and Mysto was in particularly good form that evening. He wowed them with juggling stunts and swallowing needles and performing blindfolded. After the show, he was fêted by the assembly: many bottles of vodka were consumed.

At this point the details become a bit hazy, but sometime that same night, a fierce storm blew up. Everyone was passed out or asleep when suddenly the wind ripped off the roof! Communication hook-ups were destroyed before we even had time to send an SOS. By happy accident I managed to find shelter with several other men in a chemical toilet, while the rest of the company scrambled in the worst possible confusion into the raging storm on the dark polar ice-cap. In these extreme conditions, all but two men perished within hours.

One of the survivors was Professor Tsk-tek, a native Inuit by birth and marine biologist trained at the University of Edinburgh who spoke six languages and understood the region intimately. The other was our intrepid conjurer, Mr. Mysto.

Mysto and Tsk-tek lived through the storm by huddling together for warmth and, at Tsk-tek's bidding, observing an ancient survival custom of breaking off their frozen toes and offering them to the other to eat, for energy.

But by morning enormous fissures in the ice had opened between them and the base camp toilet, cutting them off from civilization. What to do?

Thus began the most miraculous polar trek in history. These two men picked themselves up and began to walk the black ice on top of the earth, without maps, instruments or any means to measure their progress—without toes, even!—they simply walked, to keep from freezing, with no reasonable hope, no prospect beyond the menace of coming nightfall.

But bravely they continued, icicles hanging out of their nostrils, bones cracking in their joints with a sound like fire.

When suddenly, they stopped. Mysto blinked, unable to believe his eyes.

"Who is that?" He pointed. "*What* is that?"

Standing atop a crystalline glacier outcrop stood a towering figure with brick-red fur and a craggy beard like a frozen waterfall.

"Wooh—aaah!" it said.

"What is it?" Mysto insisted.

Professor Tsk-tek's voice quavered. "It's a giant yeti. I'd always wondered if the stories were true. We'd better not get any closer. It's very dangerous."

"Amazing!" said Mysto. "I could use him in my act."

He stepped forward even as Tsk-tek tried to hold him back.

"*WOOH—AHHH!*"

"It's all right, fella. I just want to—"

The yeti bared its teeth and beat its chest and suddenly, ice cracked all around. There was a sound of frigid air breaking, the dome of the sky shattering. Mr. Mysto and Professor Tsk-tek cried out, prostrating themselves on the ground.

"*OOH! OOH! OOH!*"

The ice beneath them began to sliver. And then, with a sickening slowness, a jagged black crack opened up and Mysto slid helplessly into the crevice. His last glimpse upward was of Tsk-tek clinging desperately to the edge and of two red hairy arms hoisting the Professor back to the surface.

Air whistled in Mysto's ears. He fell and fell. "I was going down for at least half a minute," he recalled. "I thought it was all over." Eventually he hit water, instantly crushing his coccyx to a powder on impact.

Even so, he managed to keep presence of mind to swim backwards while sucking the air from the small space where the water and ice met (the famous Houdini technique, long a favorite of CIA men), till he found a break in the ice-cap and resurfaced. He floated adrift on an ice-berg for three days, sustaining himself by breaking off and eating his ears, distracting himself by experimenting a new routine on a curious puffin, till he was spotted by a Norwegian whaler which rescued him and brought him to safety.

"I can't stop thinking about Tsk-tek," he later told me, at an emotional reunion in Trondheim. "The Professor was never found! Whatever happened to him and the giant yeti? No one knows. It's unexplainable. But I saw it. I was there."

I've escaped from any number of straitjackets in my day, professionally and otherwise. Any master magician practices the wiles of an escape artist: it is a tradition going back to Houdini.

Over the years I've escaped from handcuffs, chains and zip-ties. In Providence, Rhode Island, I escaped from a tuba and once, for a Shriners' Convention in Atlantic City, from a giant olive, which, despite the general bonhomie of the occasion, proved one of my most perilous exploits when I was almost mortally overcome by the fumes of that very oversized martini.

*Risk goes with the business, and I have broadcast it far and wide: **Blast does not back down from a challenge!***

I never met Houdini but, if I had, it is possible that he might have performed this trick and then lost its secret. Hence the title, which always figures prominently in my printed programs.

EFFECT:

With the help of a pair of volunteers from the audience, the performer is tied up with ropes, bound and wound with loop after loop. He can't even move. Then, moments later, sitting calmly in a chair with a sly grin on his puss and with no sign of struggle beyond a provocatively erotic squirm, the ropes suddenly fall away, and he leaps up dances a jig around his stunned captors. Oh, how the audience roars with delight!

METHOD:

The secret is in the chair. The back of the chair has a razor-sharp, spring-loaded knife, à la switch-blade, which is activated by squeezing your ankles against the lower rungs. After applying this pressure, the knife flicks out. If you lean back and make a steady motion (audiences like to see you squirm), you can cut through the ropes and thereby free yourself.

This technique requires a little practice—don't lean back too far, or you'll regret it!

Once, during a holiday when we were vacationing in Nebraska, Mrs. Blast was watching *Wheel of Fortune* and she forgot that she was sitting on my stage prop. She got a little too comfortable and it was a very unpleasant surprise.

Fortunately the doctors in the emergency ward at Omaha's Bergan Mercy Hospital are real pros. I recommend them!

1. *Pull rope baubles on lower rungs of chair together by sqeezing ankles together*

2. *This will result in triggering the switchblade mechanism*

THE ULTIMATE HIPSTER

EFFECT:

Pulling a rabbit out of a hat is, let's face it, a cliché. Likewise the appearance of fluttering doves from a silk foulard. Generations ago, when clothes were baggy and a vest with waistcoat and pochettes under the jacket were standard attire, a performer like the great Alexander Herrmann used to walk on stage with any number of rabbits concealed on his person, ducks too, and sometimes even a small deer.

Today's snugger fashions preclude such devices. The hip post-modern conjurer, though often sporting a Mephistophelean goatee, will perform while wearing little more than jeans, a T-shirt, and a few ironic tattoos.

How is it, then, that while casually strolling across stage, you clap your hands—and suddenly you are flanked by two hippopotamuses! The audience gasps. Where on earth did they come from? How marvelous!

And to be frank: how they envy you!

For tips about hippopotamus hygiene and maintenance, see the "Glossary of the Amazing" at the end of this volume.

METHOD:

It is a little-known fact that the rear-end of a hippopotamus resembles the arm of an oversized Bauhaus-design couch. (If you're thinking Weimar circa 1923, you're absolutely right!) If two hippopotamuses are positioned on either side of a settee-bench and stand very still, they blend in perfectly with the zeitgeist.

Obtain and train two hippopotamuses to stand very still. When the curtain rises at the beginning of your performance, the audience will *think* that your stage décor is a making a tasteful and trendy statement about a crucial step in modernist design kraftwerk. You should do nothing to disabuse them of the illusion.

Proceed with your show as usual. At a certain point, usually about ten to fifteen minutes into the performance, at least one of the hippopotamuses will get restless and begin to snort and snuffle.

This is your cue to stroll across stage. Don't stop what you're saying or doing but don't dawdle, either, because you don't want to make a hippopotamus wait too long. (It gets cranky.) Just be natural.

When you are in front of the "couch," clap your hands. The beasts, if properly trained, will hear this as their cue to turn around.

From there, the effect takes care of itself, and is often enhanced if, as frequently happens, the hippopotamuses are so bored that they yawn. This is delightfully theatrical. People love to see a hippopotamus yawn.

It's cool, the last word in aloof attitudinizing.

Try it!

WOK ON THE WILD SIDE

People love cooking shows, and they love to see magicians perform impossible levitations. The appeal of this feat is that you combine the two pleasures, for a wondrous best of both worlds! All this is accomplished without wires, pulleys, or gimmicked hoops.

EFFECT:

Suddenly, while demonstrating to the audience your recipe for a delicious stir fry, you flap your arms and fly around the room! *Astonishing*. Jaws will drop and, in some cases, spectators will actually fall out of their chairs.

METHOD:

The secret is in the spice. After adding your peppers and onion and garlic, you announce, "And now, for a couple of choice chilis!" Unbeknownst to observers, you also have a select moreno mushroom on your chopping board, which is included in the mix.

The moreno mushroom has wonderful hallucinogenic qualities, and can be obtained from Hopi shamans. The moreno grows on the scat of the desert dung beetle at the foot of giant cacti during their flowering season. If you don't know a Hopi shaman, you can always take Route 66 and check out the scene behind the parking lot of the Black Cat Bar in Seligman, Arizona. Tell them Blast sent you. (Cash only.) *

As your wok sizzles and you add the chilis and mushrooms, you casually remark how hot it is, cooking up a storm, so you turn on a

---

Do not try to use peyote instead of the moreno. I have conducted experiments with the entertainment possibilities of giving my audience peyote, but have learned, to my dismay, that the side effects of hot sweats and vomiting were not suitable in magic venues. At least I think it was the peyote.

nearby fan. This blows all the fumes of the mushroom toward the audience. These fumes are very potent (be sure to stand to the side!) and the front row especially will be very much affected. (When possible, seatbelts are advisable, lest they fall over and hurt themselves.)

Once the fumes start to spread, all you have to do is leave the wok on medium heat (flip once or twice, to avoid scorching) and, when you notice faces going slack and shoulders slumping, move to the side of the stage and flap your arms, for the sake of verisimilitude. The influence of the drug will do the rest—people will see you going all over the place! Usually twenty or thirty seconds suffices, then you can go back to your cooking station and turn off the fan and the heat.

IMPORTANT: Avoid exposing your audience to fumes for more than a minute. Otherwise things get sloppy, and after the show people will come backstage and want to worship you. This might seem amusing at first but it quickly becomes tedious.

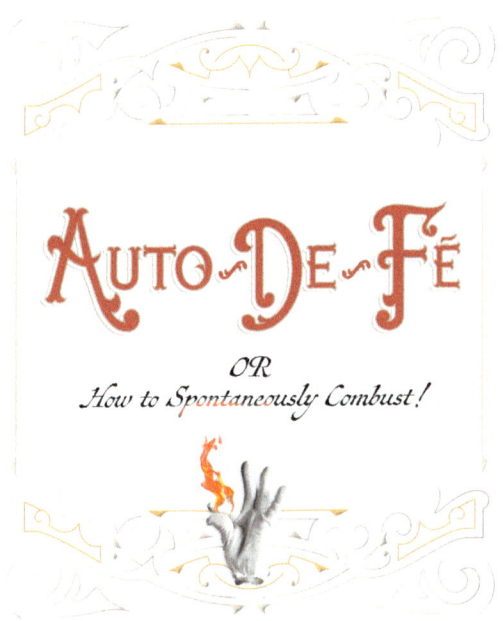

AUTO DE FÉ

OR
How to Spontaneously Combust!

Self-immolation isn't for everyone and it's one of those things that, if you're going to do it, it's worth doing right. Properly handled, though, fire is great fun and is a very satisfying medium for the working conjurer.

Effect:

Suddenly, in the middle of a witty banter with a member of the audience ("*What do you mean, you don't want to pick a card? Why, that makes me so upset I could just...*"), you burst into flames!

Method:

The secret is in your suit, which has been soaked in a n°2 blue dye injected with propane. Your clothes are thus full of tens of thousands of microbubbles of flammable gas. Cunningly, though, you have also pretreated the suit with a flame retardant. Once ignited, the gas will burn off instantly, spectacularly, in a matter of seconds, while the material of the suit itself will remain unharmed.

In your firesuit you may walk around normally as you perform your act or otherwise go about your business, but out of prudence you should not smoke or lean against a heat radiator.

When the time is right, you can detonate yourself by simply flicking a lighter in your pocket. I do so under the pretext of replacing a pack of cards in my jacket, a natural gesture...then suddenly, *Poof!*

Once ablaze, you should gesticulate and scream and shake, for maximum effect. When the flames begin to subside, you can fall to the floor and curl up like a cinder. Wait several seconds, so that the audience can take it all in. But before anyone in the audience has time to call 911, you rise to your feet, phoenix-like, triumphant! Oh, what a wonder!

FINAL REMARKS: Safety first, I always say, so I strongly suggest adding fire retardant to your eyebrows, facial hair or false whiskers, too, depending on your style. Female conjurers with long hair will naturally require a larger dose.

Sometimes, for children's shows, I perform a thematically similar version of this trick called "Riled Rumpelstiltskin" in which I feign terrible anger and split myself in half. This requires much practice, though, and is only for advanced magicians. The method is not revealed in this volume.

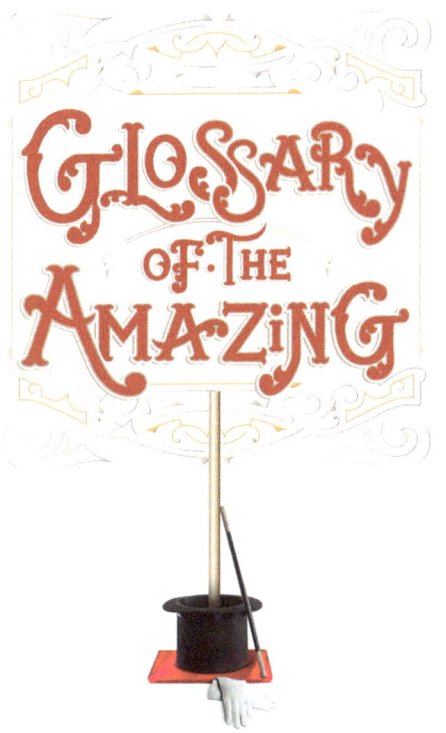

GLOSSARY OF·THE AMAZING

Assistant, *skimpily attired:* This out-of-date practice is usually associated with sexist objectification of women and should be avoided. Although early in my career Mrs. Blast used to appear onstage with me in a bikini (Mrs. Blast, not me—it was a tasteful magenta two-piece), nowadays our society has outgrown such sensibilities, just as Mrs. Blast has outgrown her bikini. (I still keep it in a private drawer, though...)

Cheshire grin: a fun way to engage your audience after a successful trick or a lively sally. Look at your spectators and begin to grin *very slowly*. Instead of a disappearance, as with Lewis Carroll's cat, the originality here arises from your grin's slow *appearance*. With practice I have learned to draw out my slow grin to several minutes. Once, at a performance in Baltimore, an elderly lady was so unnerved by my slow-motion grin that she began to weep and had to be led out of the auditorium. The air was charged!

Entrance, *making it dramatic:* your arrival on stage should include at least a drumroll and a clash of cymbals. Dry-ice smoke is optional, but remember: you are the focus of all eyes, the cynosure of desire.

Groupies: They are inevitable. Uninitiated outsiders are quickly starstruck by a prestidigitators and, in my case, given my personal magnetism, backstage moments are highly electric, even explosive. I do not presume to tell other people how to live, but I can say, based on personal experience, tears and lawsuits, that you should think twice before inviting an admirer to fondle your rabbits. Performers are only human and, before you know it, it's straight to the trap door.

On the other hand, it's true that people have to learn these things for themselves. It does get lonely on the road.

Hippopotamus, *hygiene thereof:* a practical consideration for anyone who performs "The Ultimate Hipster." Hippos love water but throwing pails over them quickly becomes tiring and most motel chains are uncooperative. That is why I suggest a large roll of quarters and a trip to the local car wash.

Fruitcakes: should not be included in preparation of hippopotamus kibble. It loosens their stool.

Improvisation: a sometime necessary expedient when a trick goes wrong or an audience does not react as anticipated. Even the most skilled performers, like myself, will on occasion be obliged to resort to improvisation. Once, after a bad night, a group of angry Norwegian peasants with sharpened birch sticks chased me from one end of their village to another with the express purpose of throwing me into a pit of quicklime. That was a tough crowd. Fortunately, I was able to slip away undetected into the long polar night.

Make-up: is not obligatory for performers. When the mood strikes me, I wear a wig, kohl eye-liner and false whiskers. Usually, though, I face the public *au naturel*.

Mesmerize: Not to be confused with *hypnotize*. You hypnotize a sentient being (see "The Incredible Talking Goldfish"); you *mesmerize* an object. (E.g., an orange or a semi-automatic weapon, though be careful with the latter when performing for Americans, because they are fragile people who easily feel infringed.)

Good conjuring requires proper English usage. There is a reason your teacher sneered at you in school.

Pharaonic Headdress: A fashion option, like a fez or rice paddy hat (conical, preferably Lao), can add a multicultural flavor to your performance. For instance, a popular variation of "Houdini's Lost Secret" can be done in pharaonic headdress. (This version is called "Tut Tut.") Instead of using ropes, you invite the volunteers to swathe you in strips of linen. People adore mummies. But, like a Second Dynasty High Priest precursor of Houdini, you shrug off your swaddlings!

Sack o' Snakes: A fun prop for children's shows. Insert a large coil into a pillowcase, large enough that you must bend the coil to close the top. Tie the top with a length of rope. This, you tell your audience, is your serpent stockpile. A shake or even a little prod will unleash the torsion of the spring until it assumes another position. How the bag jumps! How the kiddies shout!

Wand, *Magic:* An indispensable piece of equipment which adds that extra touch of mystery, the debonair aura which is central to all things Blastish. I prefer a mahogany shaft with polished nickel tips or, when the mood strikes me, a blue steel model with titanium fittings. (Warning: this can wreak havoc at airport security, so be sure to have your paperwork at the ready!) A wand can also serve as a cudgel, which comes in handy in tight situations and in the company of the impertinent.

. . . .

. . . .

These pieces first appeared,
sometimes in different form,
in the following magazines:

"The Amazing Sticking Quarter" in *The Newer York Book III*

"The Incredible Talking Goldfish" in *Calibanonline*

"Ultimate Hipster" and "Holy Cappuccino"
in *Electronic Encyclopedia of Experimental Literature*

"Wok on the Wild Side" in *Calibanonline* and *Glib*

. . . .

Special thanks
to
Royce Becker and John Carney

Charles Holdefer is the author of *Dick Cheney in Shorts* (stories), *George Saunders' Pastoralia: Bookmarked* (nonfiction) as well as four novels. His work has appeared in the *New England Review, North American Review, Chicago Quarterly Review, Slice* and elsewhere, and has been included in the Pushcart Prize anthology. He also writes essays and reviews.

www.charlesholdefer.com

www.ingramcontent.com/pod-product-compliance
Lightning Source LLC
Chambersburg PA
CBHW040743250626
47164CB00006BA/161